JUMPED IN

WILLIAM KOWALSKI

RAVEN BOOKS
an imprint of
ORCA BOOK PUBLISHERS

Library and Archives Canada Cataloguing in Publication

Kowalski, William, 1970–, author
Jumped in / William Kowalski.
(Rapid reads)

Issued in print and electronic formats.
ISBN 978-1-4598-1627-5 (paperback).—ISBN 978-1-4598-1628-2 (pdf).—
ISBN 978-1-4598-1629-9 (epub)

I. Title. II. Series: Rapid reads
PS8571.O9855J86 2017   C813'.54   C2016-907268-1
C2016-907269-X

First published in the United States, 2017
Library of Congress Control Number: 2016958169

Summary: In this work of contemporary fiction, Rasheed tries to escape
his rough neighborhood with actions both small and heroic. (RL 2.8)

*Orca Book Publishers is dedicated to preserving the environment and has
printed this book on Forest Stewardship Council® certified paper.*

Orca Book Publishers gratefully acknowledges the support for
its publishing programs provided by the following agencies:
the Government of Canada through the Canada Book Fund and the
Canada Council for the Arts, and the Province of British Columbia
through the BC Arts Council and the Book Publishing Tax Credit.

Cover design by Jenn Playford
Cover photography by iStock.com

ORCA BOOK PUBLISHERS
www.orcabook.com

Printed and bound in Canada.

20 19 18 17 • 4 3 2 1

OTHER RAPID READS BY WILLIAM KOWALSKI:

The Barrio Kings*
The Way It Works
Something Noble*
Just Gone*
The Innocence Device
Epic Game*

*Nominated for the Ontario Library Association's
Golden Oak Award

Other novels by William Kowalski:
Eddie's Bastard*
Somewhere South of Here
The Adventures of Flash Jackson
The Good Neighbor
The Hundred Hearts**
Crypt City

*Winner of the 2001 Ama-Boeke Prize

** Winner of the 2014 Thomas H. Raddall Award

ONE

You haven't seen me before, even though people like me are omnipresent.

Omni is Latin. It means "all." *Omnipresent* means "all present." Everywhere.

That's right. I'm everywhere, and yet you've never seen me. Not unless you were looking for me.

And even if you were looking for me, chances were you didn't see me anyway. I am good at not being seen. That's how I've managed to survive sixteen years so far.

I'll tell you something else about myself. It's embarrassing, but I don't care.

My favorite thing is to watch old TV shows on YouTube. I love them. *Leave It to Beaver*, *Father Knows Best*, *The Brady Bunch*. They give me this warm, cozy feeling, like everything is perfect in the world.

I know it's a lie. Everything is not perfect. But that's why I love them so much. I can pretend it's true, even though I'm smart enough not to believe it.

Watching old TV shows is what I do when I'm supposed to be at school. I figure it's safer. Just getting to school is as dangerous as running across a minefield. I have to pass by a lot of characters on the street. People talking to themselves. Gangstas with guns. Crazy people who just don't care who they hurt.

And you're not safe just because you make it to school either. Two kids got knifed there last year, one on the front steps and one in the cafeteria. Why should I risk that?

Just so I can learn how to do algebra? Uh-uh. Ain't worth it.

I'm probably learning more on YouTube anyway.

My phone is this crappy old thing I stole from somewhere. The screen is cracked, but it works fine.

I like to sit outside the 7-Eleven by my house and steal its signal. If you lean against the wall and hold your phone up high, you can get three bars. You just have to remember not to breathe through your nose. The dumpster is only ten feet away. From the way it smells, I don't think it's ever been cleaned.

I have earbuds. But I only wear one at a time. I gotta be able to hear what's going on around me. You never know when someone is going to come along and start something with you. Sometimes it's people with a beef. Sometimes it's gangstas.

Sometimes it's people who just aren't right.

There are a lot of crazy people up in this hood. Does the hood make people crazy, or do crazy people make the hood?

The old TV people live in a different universe. Their houses are clean, their neighborhoods are safe, their moms are sober, their dads exist. Everything is spotless and perfect. I like to imagine what these people would do if I just appeared in the middle of their show.

Hey, wassup! It's me, a brown-ass teenager with nappy dreads and dirty clothes. Yeah, I know it's 1950 or whatever. Y'all are surprised to see me, right? I'm from 2016, bitches. Let's talk about Barack Obama.

This is fun to think about, the same way it's fun to think about winning a million dollars.

TV people have problems, but they're all rich-white-person problems. Buddy needs to find the courage to ask a girl to prom. Little Chip or Biff breaks a window with a baseball and is worried his dad might be disappointed in him. A bunch of folks get stuck on an island and have to make all their furniture out of bamboo for the rest of their lives.

Or—my personal favorite—a dad with three boys meets some blond woman with three girls. They get married and move in together. Somehow, instead of being all crowded together and broke, now they have twice the house and twice the happiness. Because that is life in the white world.

Or so these TV shows would have you believe.

I'm not really that dumb. I know TV is fake.

My eyes are not closed. They are wide open.

If they filmed that show in my neighborhood, here's what it would look like.

The dad would be so long gone, half the kids wouldn't even remember his face. And the mom's six kids would be by five different fathers anyway. The boys would be slinging rock on the corners or running it out to the soldiers on the street. The girls would be knocked up and hanging off the shoulders of some tattooed punks who all thought they were gonna be the next 50 Cent or Diddy. Maybe some of them would be in jail, or dead. Or maybe all of them would be dead. You never know.

That's the main difference between my life and these dumbass TV shows. On TV you always know what's going to happen. No matter what crazy stuff these white people get up to, you know none of them are going to get shot over it. Back then, in their black-and-white world, the worst thing that could happen would be that one of them would get a stern talking-to. If they ever even saw a cop, it was old

Officer Friendly waving from his patrol car, returning their lost dog.

Around here, I kid you not, half the time I wake up in the morning and wonder if it's gonna be my last day on earth. If the cops show up on my street with a dog in the back, you know that dog is gonna be chewing on somebody's arm in about three seconds.

And if I see a cop, I know I need to run like hell, or my ass is gonna get beat. It doesn't matter if I didn't do anything wrong. I was walking while brown. Around here that's a crime.

Besides, I don't even *go* home. Not until I absolutely have to. Because of all the places I hate most on earth, home is number one.

TWO

Sometimes I feel like an alien scientist who's all alone on a planet of strange creatures. My job is to figure them out. Then I have to report back to my overlords.

This is the story I tell myself when I'm sitting behind the Seven, skipping school, hiding out from crackheads, trying not to get jumped in to the E Street Locals.

The E Street Locals, in case you didn't know, is the band of idiots that runs a territory in this city about three blocks square. I happen to live right in the middle of that territory.

And getting jumped in is what happens to you when you join a gang. Everyone stands around in a circle and beats the crap out of you until you fall down. If you don't die, you're in.

Real nice, huh?

The Locals think they're a gang. They're more like a collection of the greatest losers known to humanity. You know how after a rainstorm, there are little piles of trash caught up in the sewer grate? That's the Locals. They're the sewer trash of the city, stuck in the places that never get cleaned.

They would be a joke if they weren't so deadly.

The name of the leader of the Locals is Boss. Original, huh? That's the best name he can think of. He's just the latest in a long line of Locals who think they're Scarface. They keep getting arrested or killed. In two or three years, Boss will be replaced by someone else. Someone meaner and stupider.

Boss has a bunch of thugs under him. They call themselves lieutenants. I think they are giving themselves too much credit. You need brains to be a lieutenant. These guys are just mean. The worse of a person you are, the higher you rise in that gang.

The Locals sell rock and carry gats, and every once in a while they manage to shoot straight enough to kill somebody. Usually, though, if they hit you with one of their bullets, it's by accident. They don't even care if their shots go flying all over the place.

The world would be a better place without them.

If you want to avoid the E Street Locals, the best time to go out is around nine in the morning. That's because they're up all night, drinking forties and smoking weed. They usually pass out around sunrise, unless they're on a meth bender.

So if I need to bounce, that's when I go. Kinda like how on *Hogan's Heroes*, every time they escape from prison, they know just when to move to avoid the searchlights.

That's what I do this morning. I need to get out of the house. I would go back to the alley behind the Sev, but I can't deal with that reeking dumpster anymore either. I need to get out and explore. Alien scientist on the move. Expedition number nine thousand. Mission, to observe and record. Try to understand. What is the world like outside Locals territory? What would my life be like if I wasn't me?

I like to walk around the nicer parts of town, over where the university is. It's strange, because I can be there in ten minutes, but I might as well be on the moon. That's how quick things change in this city. It's like there's an invisible line— poor people on this side, rich people on that side. They don't like you to cross it. You have to wear a disguise.

I keep a backpack on so I look like a college student. I carry a notebook too. This is where I record my observations. I try not to steal too many things. Only when I absolutely can't help it or when I get hungry. I don't want to get kicked out of this world. I like it here. No one is trying to shoot me.

It's nice at the university. Big plazas, fancy buildings, lots of trees, happy-looking people. On old TV, college students are always white. Here, you see all kinds of people. They must be trying to help everybody out these days. Scholarships and shit. Money for nothing.

Maybe I can get me some of that money. I could be at home here.

I wonder what it's like to be a college student. I don't even know what I would study. I guess I need to finish high school first. I haven't been to one class all year, so I'm not sure how that's gonna happen.

But it's nice to think about. Even if it is just a pipe dream.

Pipe dream. That used to mean the dreams people had when they smoked opium through a pipe. I guess opium was the jam once. People been smoking stuff through pipes for a long time.

I guess there have always been stupid people. It's not just a new thing.

I heist myself a muffin from the student union and eat it on the library steps while I watch the people walk by. Cute girls in their prime, everywhere. I look at these girls and wonder what it takes to be their boyfriend. They probably only want a guy with lots of money and good grades. Someone from a good family. Someone who is going somewhere in life. Someone with a car.

You can't really blame them. Who wants someone who comes from nothing, has nothing to give and is going nowhere?

I got dreams, sure. Like every other kid in my neighborhood, I wanted to be a rapper. Rappers are who we all look up to—big guns, nice cars, fat stacks of cash, hot chicks all over. I don't feel that way anymore though. Too much like the gang life. I don't know what I really want anymore.

I never really had a girlfriend. There was a girl I used to like once, but she runs with the Locals now. A while back I heard she got a baby. She wasn't but fourteen.

I make some notes in my notebook. I draw a few sketches.

Then I go into the library and grab a book. I don't look to see what it is. I don't care. I'll read anything. Besides, everyone else has books out, so I need one too. You wanna fit in, you gotta do what all the other kids are doing, right?

They have couches in here. I sprawl out on one and open up my book. It turns out to be an encyclopedia. The letter *M*. I read about the mongoose.

Man, I never knew mongeese were so boring. Before you know it, I'm asleep.

No surprise there. I don't get much sleep at home, what with all the shouting and the sirens and the yelling. I tend to grab it when I can.

But this was the wrong place to fall asleep.

THREE

Next thing I know, someone is shaking me by the shoulder. He's not being any too gentle about it either.

It takes me a few seconds to wake up. Soon I realize this isn't just any somebody. It's a dude in a uniform. A cop. Maybe thirty years old, blond hair in a crew cut, square jaw. Looks like a cartoon. A real jerk. Uh-oh. Does he know about that muffin?

"Quit shakin' me," I say. "I got rights."

"You got ID?"

I pat my pockets. This is just for show. I never had any ID. ID costs money.

"Nuh-uh," I say.

"You a student here?"

"Yeah, I'm a student."

"Really." He obviously doesn't believe me.

"What, you don't think a punk like me can read a book? Check me out." I hold up my encyclopedia.

Now everyone else in the library is looking at me. I can feel their eyes. But when I look at them, everyone looks away. Because, of course, the cop is talking to the grungy-looking brown kid. Not to the clean-cut white boys and girls who always mind their manners, who had the good sense not to be born into minorities. And the other people of color in the library don't want to get caught up in my stuff. I'm not like them either. I'm dirtier. They can tell I don't belong.

It doesn't have to be crosses burning on the lawn to be racist. It can be you just looking away.

This cop is no dummy. I haven't fooled him.

"What's your major?" he asks.

Major? Not sure what that means. Oh yeah—I saw it on TV. It means what are you studying.

"Criminal justice," I say. "I'm gonna be a cop someday."

That's a total lie, of course. Not even a very good one. I don't even know why I said it.

"Really. You, a cop."

"Hell yes."

He smirks.

"You don't even have a student ID?" he asks.

"I musta left it back in my room," I say.

"Which dorm you in?"

"Huh?"

"Which dorm?"

I think fast. What the hell is a *dorm*? I have no idea. It sounds like some kind of bug.

Dorm. Dorm. Wait. He must mean where my room would be. Oh, *dormitory*. From the Latin word for "sleeping room."

See? I do read.

"I'm on the third floor," I say.

"Yeah, but which building?"

"Aren't you in Meem?" says a voice.

We both turn and look, me and the cop. There's a pretty white girl standing there. She's got one of those perky little white-girl noses that turns up at the end like a ski jump. The rest of her is pretty perky too. Damn. *Damn*.

"Yeah, Meem," I say. "That's it. Meem is the place to go for all your dorming needs. I wouldn't dorm anywhere else. Meem all the way."

"I'm his resident assistant," the girl says to the cop. "He must have forgotten his ID again. He's always doing that." She turns to me. "How many times have I told you, uh…"

I turn to the cop and hold my hand out.

"Darius Higgenbotham," I say. "How do you do." This is how white people act, see. I know this. Watching all those shows was better than college.

"...Darius Higgenbotham," says the perky girl.

"Higgenbotham?" says the cop. He looks skeptical. *Really* skeptical.

I shrug. I hope he doesn't ask me to spell it, because I just made it up on the spot. My name ain't no Darius Higgenbotham. What you call me depends on who you are to me. My mom calls me Baby, but if you call me that I'll pop your ass.

"All right," he says. "Darius Higgenbotham. Try to remember your ID next time, okay? Students are supposed to carry it at all times."

"I will, Officer."

"See you, Lanaia," says the cop.

"See you, Officer Townsend," says the perky Lanaia.

He walks away. Lanaia and I stand there and stare at each other for a minute. Well, I stare. She just kind of looks.

"Thanks," I say.

She nods. "No problem," she says.

I want to ask her why she did that. But suddenly I'm feeling shy. I'm not sure what happens next.

I've seen shows like this. White girl meets brown boy, lifts him up out of the gutter. I don't need to be anyone's social experiment. If she tries to uplift me, I'm gonna tell her to go work out her white guilt on someone else. Although maybe I'll try to get a few dates with her first.

But none of that happens. She just kind of smiles and walks away.

And after another minute, so do I.

Why did she help me out? Why? I need to know.

FOUR

Sometimes I have to go home, even though I don't want to.

But I need to check in and see that my sister, Daneeka, is okay.

I already know the answer to that. She's not okay. She'll never be okay. But I feel like I have to check in on her anyway.

Daneeka's got my mom there with her, but my mom is not okay either. She's what you call chronically depressed.

Notice a common theme here? Nobody in my life is okay.

Some people on this alien planet use *chronic* as a slang term for weed. They so dumb, they don't even know what it really means.

Chronic comes from the ancient Greek word *chronos*, meaning "time." It means "long-lasting or permanent." You chronically depressed, you ain't about to just pop a pill and start bouncing around the room. *Chronically depressed* means you got serious stuff on your mind. And it's there to stay.

Moms is also a drug addict. If she was white, they would say she is "self-medicating." But when you're black, you just a pill-popper. She stays in her room most of the time. I don't know what she does in there. I don't like to go in. It smells bad.

Daneeka, my sister, is usually in one of two places, in front of the computer or the television. Today it's the computer.

Now you may be wondering, *how did this poor-ass ghetto kid get a TV and a computer? He made it sound like he practically lives in a box.*

Insurance money. Government money. That's how. Not mine. Daneeka's.

She's the one who got shot, after all. I guess you could say she earned it.

When I walk in the front door, she turns around in her wheelchair and gives me a big superhero welcome. Same thing every time, like she hasn't seen me in ten years. Does she really feel that way about me? I wonder. Or is it all part of her bigger problem, the one that makes her see the world like she's nine years old, even though she's going on nineteen?

"Hey, Neeks," I say to her. That's my nickname for her.

"Baby brother!" she shrieks. "Oh my god! Look at you!"

"Yeah, look at me," I say. "You just saw me this morning."

"I still can't believe how big and tall you are."

"Really. Even though you been seeing me every day for sixteen years."

"Such a fine, handsome boy!"

"You need anything, Neeks?"

"No, I'm good. Where you been?"

"School, Neeks. I been at school all day."

"Uh-huh. Learn anything?"

"Yeah. A whole bunch."

"Tell me something!" She claps her hands and opens her eyes real wide. I hate this playacting. But you can't talk sense to Neeks anymore. Something inside her is broken. Something besides her spine, I mean.

I shrug.

"Recent discoveries have proven that gravity is made of particles called gravitons," I say. I saw this on YouTube. I don't really know what it means, but it sounds cool.

Gravity comes from the Latin *gravis*, meaning "heavy." I love reading about the history of words. All this stuff is online. That's how I know that if it wasn't for those old Latin dudes, we would hardly have any words at all. We would just point at things and go *ook, ook*.

Neeks looks like she is going to cry.

"I am so proud of you," she whispers.

"Yeah, thanks, Neeks."

My sister is very pretty. If she wasn't in a wheelchair, she'd have a dozen boyfriends. But she's been stuck in that chair for the past ten years, and she's never getting out. And for that reason, guys don't come around here.

When she was nine years old, my sister was lying in bed, asleep, when a .45-caliber bullet came through the wall and struck her in the spine. It shattered two of her vertebrae, and it almost killed her. She was in the hospital for months. She survived, obviously, but she lost all the use of her legs. She has to go to the bathroom into a plastic bag, through a hole in her stomach. She won't ever have children. She won't ever walk again.

All of that is bad enough. But there are...other issues. It's like her brain froze on the day she was shot, and she stopped developing. Mentally, she's still a little girl. This is all what you call psychological. The bullet didn't hit her brain. But it might as well have.

A doctor explained it to us once. When a very traumatic incident happens, sometimes people just can't get past it. They stop changing then and there. It's like they're frozen on the day it happened, and they're too scared to move beyond it. They need to stay where it's safe. Even when it makes no sense, and even when it makes them look crazy. They're not crazy. They're just... scared. Permanently scared.

So that's how you get a nineteen-year-old woman with the mind of a nine-year-old girl.

Trauma is a Greek word. It means "wound." Between those Latins and Greeks giving us all their words, we basically don't even speak English.

I sort of understand. I can't imagine how scared she must have been. She claims she doesn't even remember it happening. I believe that too. She must have wiped it out of her mind. Imagine that. You go to sleep one night like normal. In the middle of the night, you wake up with blood everywhere. You're surrounded by paramedics and cops. There are sirens going off. Your mother is screaming. Somebody is probably saying something stupid like, *Everything is going to be okay*.

When someone is telling you everything is going to be okay, that's a pretty sure sign that everything is going down the crapper.

I don't remember much of that night. Neeks is three years older than I am, which means I was only six years old at the time. All I know is, my big sister has become my little sister. And it's weird.

I head back to my room.

I say this room is mine, but it doesn't feel like mine. We don't own this house. We rent it. I don't eat here, because no one ever cooks. A service brings my sister her meals. My mother doesn't seem to eat anything but my sister's pain medication. My sister doesn't need it, but she says she does so she can get more pills. So she can give them to our mother. Around and around it goes.

"Baby, that you?" comes my mother's voice from her room.

"Would you please stop calling me that?" I yell back.

"How was school?"

"Who cares how school was? Just a bunch of boring old crap anyway."

"Can you bring me some tea?"

"Get your own damn tea, junkie," I mumble. But I don't say it loud enough for her to hear me. I don't actually want to hurt her.

I just want her to stop hurting the rest of us.

I make her some tea and leave it outside her door. I just knock to tell her it's there. I don't want to see her. She looks half-dead.

I go into my room and look around. I feel less and less like I belong here. I don't own much. Just a few clothes, an old radio, a turntable and a mic I scrounged from the garbage back when I thought I was gonna become a rapper or maybe a DJ. But the turntable arm is broken, and the mic doesn't work either. Posters on the wall from when I was twelve—Kendrick Lamar, Nas, Lil Wayne. I still like these guys. K-Dot gets deeper all the time.

I stole myself some dinner from a convenience store on the way home—a sandwich wrapped in plastic, and a bag of chips. I kick back and watch more shows while I eat. The warm cozy lie creeps over me again. Everything is okay. Everything is great.

Thank God for old TV.

As I lie there falling asleep, I find myself thinking about that girl again. Lanaia. Why did she stick up for me? I need to find her again and ask her out. Maybe she's a few years older than me. Maybe she's too smart. Too white. Whatever. If I'm ever going to understand the beings on this planet, I need to investigate further. Get closer. Dig deeper. Find out what makes them do the things they do.

FIVE

Alien-scientist expedition number 9,002: Return to university campus.

Mission: Locate Lanaia, hot human girl who helped me. Possibly get phone number, so I can call her and ask her out.

Maybe steal another one of them muffins. Man, it was good. It had chocolate chips in it.

How am I going to call her? I have a phone, but no phone plan.

Never mind. I'll figure that out later.

I leave the house early in the morning. On the way back to campus, I pass two crackheads screaming at each other on the corner. One very old black man lying on a bench. He might be dead. I don't stop to check. If I see a problem, I do not get involved.

That is rule number one of the hood. Keep moving. Just keep moving.

One car full of four thugs, who pass me like a shark cruising a swimmer.

In this hood, you get real good real fast at telling from a distance what color of clothing people are wearing. I can see from a thousand miles away that these guys are wearing the white T-shirts and black do-rags of the Locals.

And I can see that Boss himself is sitting in the passenger seat.

My blood turns cold. I get ready to run or fight. Not sure why I think fighting is an option. If it comes down to that, I'm dead. I won't give up, but I don't stand a chance either.

Boss and I lock eyes for a minute. Or maybe just a second. Or maybe our eyes don't meet at all, but I think they do.

He turns and says something to the guy who's driving.

The car comes screeching to a halt. Stereo so loud it upsets my stomach. Or maybe that's my fear. The music gets quieter.

Boss sticks his arm out the window and points at me. Then he beckons.

I stare at him, wishing very hard that this wasn't happening. Time stretches out, and moments become hours. I can feel my feet moving me toward him, even though I don't want to go.

I stop about ten feet away. I don't want Boss to be able to grab me. I've seen him do cruel things to people before, like drag them down the street with his car when they ain't paid what they owe. Or when they don't show the proper respect.

Boss has killed people. I'm sure of it. But the cops don't care, and no one will rat him out anyway.

I don't say anything. I just wait.

Boss is about thirty-five years old, I guess. That's old for a free gangster. Most of them are dead or doing hard time by that age. He wears a black do-rag on his bald head, and a white muscle shirt. He's got really ripped arms from working out in the prison yard, where he's spent most of his life. A scar on his forehead. Not sure I want to know how he got that.

"Sup with you, man?" says Boss. He has a real deep voice, like the rumbling of a truck.

"Sup, Boss," I say.

He gives me a long, critical look.

"Your name Rasheed, ain't it?"

"Yeah, Boss."

"Yeah, I thought so. I knowed your daddy. Who you runnin' with these days?"

35

I shrug. "Nobody," I say.

"What? Speak up, fool. Can't hear you."

"Nobody, Boss."

He looks at me for a long while.

"How come I don't see you around here much?"

I shrug again. "I like to lie low," I say. "Not bother nobody."

"You like to lie low. How you gonna feed your family, man?"

"Get a job."

"What kinda job?"

"I dunno," I say.

"You ain't goin' to school, I hear."

Now how did he hear that? Boss knows everything. That's scary.

"Naw," I say.

"So what kinda job you gonna get, you ain't been to school?"

"I dunno, Boss."

"I hear you like to read books."

"Yeah."

"Tell me what this mean. No man is an island."

Another shrug. "I dunno, Boss."

"Don't be tellin' me you dunno. Think about it. Tell me what it mean."

"It means...you gotta run with some-body," I say.

"Whassat you say?"

"You gotta run with somebody," I say again.

"That's right. Gotta run with some-body. Why you don't wanna run with us?"

I look down at my shoes.

"Ain't my life, that's all," I say.

What I really want to say is, *'Cause you're the sons of bitches who shot my sister. And you're ruining the world for everyone who lives anywhere near you.*

But I don't have that kind of courage in real life. Only in my daydreams.

"Your daddy was my boy," Boss says. "You know that?"

What he means is that he and my father were good friends. I did not know that. I wasn't going to look up at him, but I can't help myself. I stare at him in surprise.

"Really?"

"Yeah, me and him was tight. He was all right. Tough. Solid. Respect."

"Word," I say. I want to ask him if he knows where my father is. But I'm afraid of what the answer might be.

"You look just like him," he says.

I didn't know that either. My mother would never say such a thing to me. She never talks about my father.

"You gonna need a job," Boss says. "And you gonna need people too. Who you gonna hang with? Those white kids at the college you like to go to? What you think, you some kinda frat boy or something?"

He knows that too?

"You wanna be a man, you gotta be productive," says Boss. "And you wanna be productive, you gotta line yourself up with the people who make things happen around here. You understand? Otherwise, you produce nothing. And you might end up helping the wrong people."

I can feel him staring at me. I don't want to meet his eyes.

"Remember what I say," says Boss. "No man is an island."

"No man is an island, Boss," I say.

He turns to his driver. "Bounce," he says.

The stereo starts blasting again, and the car rolls down the street.

I have to check to make sure I didn't wet my pants. I just survived an encounter with the leader of the Locals.

Maybe that's enough for one day. Maybe I should just go back to bed. It's gonna be all downhill from here.

But if I go back to the university, I might get to see Lanaia again.

And no matter what happens now, it won't scare me near as much as what just happened.

SIX

It's Friday morning, about eight thirty.

Campus is a busy place. Lots of people walking to class or just sitting and talking. Everyone has a coffee in his or her hand. I figure I should get one too, but I don't want to spend the money, and you can't really steal coffee. I specialize in things that fit into my pockets. I always wear cargo pants. So many pockets, even I lose track.

I spend a lot of time looking around, waiting to see who might be spying on me. But I don't see any gangsters in black do-rags.

I don't see Lanaia anywhere either.

So I just hang. It's fun watching all these people. I check out some kids skate-boarding, grinding down the steps. They don't have a care in the world. They'll go to classes. Graduate. Get good jobs. Nice houses. Their lives are like an old TV show. Not real. Just pretend.

My life is real. Theirs is just a TV script.

I feel a tap on my shoulder. I turn around.

Aw, man. It's old Officer Friendly. The same cop who tried to kick me out of the library yesterday.

"Hey there," he says. "Remember me?"

"Sup," I say.

"Darius Higgenbotham, right?"

I try not to laugh at that.

"The one and only," I say.

"How are things in Meem?"

"Great. Just perfect."

"On your way to class?"

"Yeah, I was just headed that way now."

"You said criminal justice, right?"

"Yep."

"Well, the CJ building is on the other side of campus, you know."

"Oh, well, I'm going to a special presentation this morning," I say.

"Really?"

"Yeah. It's called How to Hassle Brown Kids for No Reason. All cops have to take it."

"Funny," says Officer Friendly.

He and I eye each other up for a few seconds.

"What you messing with me for?" I ask.

"I'm not messing with you. I'm just doing my job," he says.

"A robot could do your job," I say. "Why don't you go find some criminals to arrest? My neighborhood is full of them." Oops, I just gave myself away. "My old neighborhood, I mean, before I became a college student.

If you were a real cop, that's what you'd be doing. If there were any real cops anywhere, they'd be arresting the ones who need it. The dealers and the punks and the gangbangers. Not people who ain't buggin' anyone."

Man, I hate this dude. His prickly hair, his sunglasses, his big arms, his cocky attitude. Cops think they protect people, but all they do is strut around acting like they own the place. Make themselves feel better for having tiny dicks. He probably grew up watching NASCAR and yelling shit at black people out car windows for fun. Maybe he was in the Klan. I bet he's got a Nazi tattoo somewhere under that uniform.

"My job is to protect this campus," he says.

"If your job was being a racist, you'd be getting a medal," I say.

"What'd you say?"

"You heard me."

"You think because I'm asking you questions, I'm a racist?"

"Well, I don't see you bugging any of the other people around here."

"That's because they all belong here. They go to school here. What's your story?"

"I told you. Criminal justice."

"That's a funny thing to pick. If you're gonna lie, why not pick something believable?"

"'Cause black kids can't be cops?"

"That's not what I meant," he said. "You're not really a student here. You don't live in Meem. I checked. Your name isn't Darius Higgenbotham. You lied to a cop. That makes you suspicious. That right there is enough reason to arrest you."

"Fine, I'm going," I say, and I turn around and start walking.

"Wait," he says.

"What you want now?"

"Tell you what. I'll make you a deal."

I look at him for a long moment. People never try to make deals unless they think they are going to come out ahead.

"What deal?"

"A criminal-justice deal. You obviously care about law and order. You think being a cop is so easy. I bet you'd be great at it. You see those kids over there skateboarding?"

"Yeah, I see 'em."

"Here's your first criminal-justice assignment. Go over there and tell them to stop."

I laugh. "Why would I do that?"

"Because you're not allowed to skate on those steps. It's dangerous, and they're damaging private property. There's a sign right there that says *No Skateboarding*. See it?"

"Yeah, I see it." Maybe I was wrong about this guy. Maybe he's not trying to put one over on me. Maybe he's just nuts.

"So, let's see you strut your stuff."

"Man, you crazy. I ain't about to go over there." Stupid white-people rules. *No Skateboarding*. Is he serious? Who cares about skateboarding? Maybe they should put up signs in my neighborhood that say *No Crack Dealing. No Gangbanging. No Shooting Nine-Year-Old Girls In The Back*. Signs about things that matter. If illegal skateboarding is the biggest problem these people have to deal with, they don't know how good they got it.

"Why not?" he says.

"Because I don't care if they skate. Besides, you think they gonna listen to me?"

"Why wouldn't they listen to you?"

"Look at me! I ain't even got a uniform on."

"It's not about the uniform," says Officer Friendly. "It's about the way you carry yourself. It's about being assertive."

"You mean acting like a jerk," I say.

"If that's how you need to think about it."

"All right. You the expert in that. So how do you do it?"

"What you do is, you just go over there and look them in the eye. You don't try to push them around, but you don't back down either. You let them know by your body language that you mean business. And you just tell them they have to stop. You show them the sign. You tell them to move along."

"And if they don't?"

"Then you call it in."

"*Call it in*? Are you serious?"

"Yep. And you ask for their ID and you write them a ticket."

"Call it in how? On what? My phone? I ain't even got a phone plan."

"Don't let it come to that," he says. "Your job is to make them move. That is the only acceptable outcome."

These kids are older than me. Bigger than me. Richer than me. Whiter than me.

"And what if I don't?" I say.

"Well, then," says Officer Friendly, "I'm gonna kick you off this campus for good, and if I ever see you back here, I'll arrest you. Because this is private property, and it's for people who want to learn. Not people who want to scope out chicks and steal food from the student union. You ever wanna come back here again, this is the deal."

Uh-oh. I guess he saw me take that muffin yesterday.

I swallow.

"All right," I say. "Here I go."

As I approach these kids, I think, I could just keep on walking. He can't do anything to me. I could just walk off campus and go home.

But then I can't come back here anymore.

And besides, they're not supposed to be skateboarding. What is wrong with them anyway? There's a sign right there that says *No Skateboarding*. People are trying to walk up and down the stairs, and they're in the way. Making it dangerous for everyone else. Like they don't even care if they accidentally hurt someone.

If there's one thing that really pisses me off, it's people who make it dangerous for everyone else.

"Yo," I say.

The three of them ignore me. It's like I'm not even there.

"Hey. Listen up."

They stop. They look at me.

"Yeah?" says one.

"You can't skate here, yo," I say.

There is a very long silence. I swear you can hear the wind blowing through my dreads.

"*What*?" says one of them.

"There's a sign right there says so."

The three of them look at the sign. They look at me. Clearly they don't believe what they are seeing and hearing.

"So?"

"Ya'll are being a nuisance," I say. "People trying to walk up and down these steps, and they have to go around you. It ain't right. So take off. Get outa here with them things."

"Or what?" says one of the skaters.

"Or I'm gonna call 9-1-1 on your asses and get you some tickets, that's what," I say. "Choice is yours."

They look at each other. Then back at me. This goes on for about twenty seconds.

"Okay, bro," says one. "Chill out."

Then they pick up their boards and start to walk away.

I stand there and watch them go. I can't quite believe what I'm seeing.

I look back at Officer Friendly. He's half hiding behind a tree. He's smiling at me like he can't believe it either. He gives me a big thumbs-up.

What a weird day this is turning out to be.

SEVEN

"So what's your real name?" Officer Friendly asks me.

"Rasheed," I say.

"Well, Rasheed, you were great," says Officer Friendly. "A real natural."

We're sitting in the student union. Officer Friendly has bought me some french fries. He's having a water. Got to keep his manly figure. Me, I could live off french fries. I eat and eat and never gain weight.

"Thanks," I say. The fries here are pretty good. I look around as I eat them. Lots of people are looking at us, trying to figure it out.

What is that cop doing with that punk? I'm trying to figure it out too.

"So how did it feel?"

I shrug.

"Okay, I guess," I say.

"Just okay?"

"Pretty good, actually."

"Why?"

"What you mean, why?"

"Why did it feel good?"

"I dunno, man. What's with all the questions?"

"I'm trying to get you to do a little self-reflection," says the good officer. "Don't act like I'm pulling teeth or something."

Self-reflection. Gah. I had a teacher last year who was always asking us to write papers about self-reflection. Every time you tied your shoe, he wanted you to reflect on the experience and then write five hundred words about it. It drove me crazy. I hate self-reflection.

But I decide to humor him.

"It felt good because…I felt like I helped."

He nods. "Helped how?"

"Helped keep people safer," I say. "Maybe just a little bit. But that's better than doing nothing."

"Were you scared?"

"A little. Not really."

"Why not?"

"Well, I knew you were right there. If I yelled, you would come."

He nods. "And now you just learned another lesson," he says. "The importance of backup."

"You ever have backup?"

He shakes his head and grins.

"Not me," he says. "I'm a cowboy. Only time I ever get to ask for help is in a dangerous situation, like if someone has a weapon."

"Does that ever happen to you?"

"Not yet. But it could."

"So when you got to tell people to do something, you're on your own. And you have to hope they listen."

"Not hope," he says. "I make sure they listen. Try not to leave anything to chance."

I finish my fries.

"You still hungry?" he asks.

"Come on, man, you embarrassing me," I say. "I'm not some starving African kid."

"You wouldn't eat a hamburger?"

"Well…"

Five minutes later, I'm tearing into a hamburger.

"So where do you really live?" he says.

I tell him the name of my intersection. He nods.

"Rough part of town," he says.

"No cops around there," I say. "We got bigger problems than skateboarding."

"You have family?"

I tell him about my sister and my mom. I leave out the part about my mom being a drug addict. No need to fill every stereotype today.

"So how come you hang around here?"

"I wanna go to college someday," I say.

I'm surprised to hear myself say that. I never said that out loud before. I never even let myself think it. But he doesn't laugh at me or look surprised. He just nods again.

"I figured that was it," he says. "I knew when you told me criminal justice that you were a man with a plan."

"Come on, bro," I say. "I was just straight up gassin' you. I never wanted to be no criminal-justice major. I never even thought about it. Not once."

"And yet you said it," Officer Friendly says. "You didn't hesitate. You just said it."

"So?"

"So I think you were telling the truth. You really do want to make the world a safer place."

"Yeah, maybe," I say.

"Starting with your neighborhood. Am I right?"

He looks at me. I'm surprised to feel myself getting hot behind the eyes, like they're about to start leaking. Damn, is this dude some kind of wizard? I duck my head down and pretend to blow my nose into a napkin. Because for some reason, when he said that my thoughts went right to my sister.

"Well, hey there," says Officer Friendly. "How are you today, Lanaia?"

Oh no. Not now. The worst possible time.

"Hi there, Officer Townsend," says Lanaia. She's got a stack of books in her arms, and she's looking as perky as ever. "Hi, Darius!"

"Hi," I mumble.

"What are you guys up to?"

"We were just talking about criminal justice," says Officer Friendly.

"Great!" says Lanaia. "Listen, I have to run. I'm late. I just wanted to say hi. Nice to see you guys are friends now."

Today is the kind of day when I feel like I can do anything. Did I not just run a bunch of older skate punks off the steps? I am no longer just plain old Rasheed. I am Darius Higgenbotham, unstoppable avenger of justice.

"Don't leave yet, girl. I need your digits," I say.

Officer Townsend stares at me as if I just started speaking ancient Greek. So does Lanaia. Then she bursts out laughing.

I feel myself starting to blush. Why did I even say that? It busted out of me before I had time to think. I never was too good at controlling my mouth.

"Okay, Darius," she says. "Since you asked, here you go." She takes out a scrap of paper and a pen from her purse, writes her number down, hands it to me. "Gotta respect a man who knows what he wants," she says.

And then she leaves.

Officer Townsend is shaking his head like he can't believe what just happened.

"I have no clue how you just pulled that off, but I gotta give it up to the master," he says. "That was slick."

"I got a way with the ladies," I say. I don't want him to see I'm just as shocked as he is.

"She likes you, man. She stuck up for you yesterday in the library too. She thought you were being treated unfairly."

"I *was* being treated unfairly."

"Oh, really? So you really are a student here, and you weren't trespassing?"

He's got me there.

"What do I do?" I say.

"What do you mean, what do you do? You call her."

"Yeah, but...then what?"

"Don't you think you better start by telling her your real name?" he says.

"Yeah," I say. "That would be a good start."

EIGHT

There's only one way I'll be able to call Lanaia, and that's if I get a phone plan.

I can't afford a real plan. But I can get a card with prepaid minutes.

For that I need at least ten bucks. Maybe twenty.

So how do I get twenty bucks?

In my neighborhood, there's one way to get money, and that's to work for the Locals. But that's not the kind of work you can do on a part-time basis. And you can never quit. Once you're in, you're in.

The Locals have been trying to get me to join them since I was a kid. They have runners as young as eight or nine years old. These kids never had a chance at a normal life. They'll be in and out of juvy and prison until they die too young. Along the way they're going to get hurt a lot. And they're probably going to hurt a lot of people.

That was my dad's life story. He grew up in this neighborhood. This was before crack got big, but things were still rough. I heard enough stories to know what it was like. A lot of turf wars with other gangs, both black and Mexican. And always fighting with the cops.

I never knew my daddy too well, but I knew he was a Local. Back when it was actually something to be proud of.

I don't remember much about him. But I remember him telling me once that gangs were not there just to cause trouble. They were there to protect people. When everything around you was on fire, and you had no one else looking out for you, you had to stick together. You and your people. That's what gangs were first—protection. A family.

It's been a long time since the Locals had that kind of honor. Now they're just a bunch of wasted punks.

I wish I knew which one of them fired the gun that hit my sister and ruined her life. All of our lives. So many nights I lie awake in bed, filled with anger, listening to them whoop it up outside like they don't have a care in the world. Shooting off their guns. My sister lying in her own bed, crying in fear. Worried another bullet is going to come for her and finish the job.

No wonder my mom is on the pills. How could a normal person take this kind of life? It's no different than living in a war zone.

Only no one is ever coming to save you. You're stuck, forever. No one cares.

I wish for the millionth time I could make a lot of money real fast. I would get us the hell out of this neighborhood.

What would I do if I could find the one who shot my sister?

Criminal justice. That's what.

Next morning I wake up still thinking about twenty dollars.

There's milk in the fridge that's still good. Cereal. I make breakfast for myself. The meal-delivery service comes with Daneeka's breakfast. They drop it at the door, ring the bell and leave fast. I've never actually seen these people. I'm surprised they still even come into this neighborhood. But the Locals leave them alone too. They don't carry money, and their food isn't worth stealing. Daneeka's Medicare pays for it. It tastes like cardboard. No one would want to steal that.

I bring Neeks her tray and put her old one back on the steps. The service will pick it up when they come with her lunch. Neeks and I have the same conversation we have every morning. We ask how the other slept. She asks what I will do that day. I lie. It's like talking to a recording.

My mom comes out of her room to use the bathroom, grabs a few pills, goes back inside. She doesn't say a word to either of us. She smells like she needs to shower.

Just a normal morning in my house.

What would people on old TV do if they needed twenty dollars?

I think about all the episodes I've seen. They would hold a car wash. Or a bake sale. Or form a singing group and enter a contest.

Screw that. All those things would get me shot around here.

I end up earning it the old-fashioned way.

I head to the main drag and walk up and down until I pass a lady who isn't paying close enough attention to her purse. It's simple to reach in and help myself to her wallet. She doesn't even notice. I am that good.

I hold the wallet close until I'm around the corner. Then I stop, lean against the wall and check it out. A few credit cards. I won't touch those. Too easy to trace. Three worn twenties and a handful of change. Well, she wasn't a millionaire. But more than I need.

I toss her wallet in a sewer. Then I buy a phone card from a convenience store. With the money left over, I get myself a real breakfast at a diner. Scrambled eggs, pancakes and bacon. I don't get to eat like this too often.

I don't feel bad about stealing. There is the law, and then there is justice.

Just because some things are illegal doesn't mean they're wrong. What's wrong is that some people have so much while others have so little. Sometimes a little stealing can actually make things right again.

I know old Officer Friendly wouldn't see it that way. But he doesn't understand my life. Fine, so he's not the hardass I thought he was. He took the time to sit and talk with me. Then he probably went home and told his wife what a great guy he was for giving food to a poor black kid.

I don't need charity. I need a break.

I punch in the card number. Then I call Lanaia's phone. I've never called a girl like this. I feel like I have two pit bulls fighting in my stomach.

She doesn't answer. Dang. Maybe it's too early. I'm thinking about hanging up, but I hear her voice, all chipper and perky, telling me to leave her a message. So I do. I don't even know what I say. Something stupid.

My brain stops working. Talking to girls is hard.

I head out of the restaurant and down the street. I'm not going anywhere special, so I'm in no hurry. Maybe back to my hideout behind the Seven. Maybe somewhere new. Definitely not home.

A few minutes later I get a text.

Hey wassup it's me Lanaia

I write back, **Hi how you doin**

Good how bout you

Then my thumbs pause in midair. What am I supposed to say next? I already asked her how she's doing. I didn't come with a game plan. Normally I'm a take-it-as-it-comes kind of guy. But suddenly I have no clue what to do. I'm glad we're texting and not talking. Otherwise this would have turned into a very long and awkward silence.

She decides to go next.

Can I ask you a question

yes im single and available, I text back. I'm walking along, not looking where I'm going, just a typical kid in the city. No reason for the cops to hassle me, right?

Ha ha ha that was not my question

Okay go ahead

How old are you?

Uh-oh. You know when a chick is using proper capitalization and punctuation, she ain't messin'.

I'm just debating what my answer should be when I hear a *whoop, whoop.* This is the sound that sends a cold dagger of fear through the heart of every black teenaged boy in this city.

"Keep your hands where we can see them," says a voice through a loudspeaker.

It's the five-o.

I'm about to get ten-fiftied.

NINE

If you're white, let's be honest. You probably don't even know what a ten-fifty is.

If you're black, let's be even more honest. No two numbers in the English language will make you more nervous.

Ten-fifty is the name of the form the police use when they conduct random stops. They're allowed to stop people, anytime, anywhere, search them and ask them questions. They fill out a ten-fifty form and keep it on file. That way, if you ever get arrested in the future, they already have all kinds of dirt on you they can trot out in court. *See, Your Honor? He's not the innocent victim he makes himself out to be. Look at how many times we had to talk to him!*

The idea is, it's supposed to make the city safer. Of course, what this usually means is that black kids get stopped constantly, while white kids get left alone. I know black kids who have been ten-fiftied twenty or thirty times. I knew white kids at my school last year who had never been ten-fiftied once in their lives.

I ain't trying to make it racist. I'm just saying. This is the way it is.

You're supposed to be able to decline a ten-fifty and keep going. We all know what really happens to people who do that. They develop a sudden case of handcuffs, and on their way to the station they probably get slapped around a lot. Cops hate it when you make them work for a living.

"Just stay right there," says the cop who is getting out on the driver's side. This cop is white. Beefy, crew cut, mustache.

Another cop is getting out of the passenger side. This one is black. Bald head, huge arms. Tattoos.

You might think I'd be happy to see a black cop. Uh-uh. They're even worse than the white ones sometimes. Almost like they're trying to show their white buddies they don't play favorites. A black cop might be less likely to shoot a black kid. But he'll be ten times more likely to kick your ass just for fun. I know. It's happened to me more than once. And I'm really hoping it doesn't happen again today.

"Take your backpack off and set it on the ground," says the black cop.

I do it.

"What's that in your hand?" asks the white one, like maybe his eyes aren't working.

"My phone," I say.

"Yeah? Lemme see it."

"It's my phone," I say. "I ain't gotta let you see it."

"Why not? Who were you texting, your dealer?"

"You mind if I go through this bag?" says the black cop, and he picks up my backpack and opens it. This is how they work. They ask you a lot of questions real quick and hope you make a mistake. "Anything in here that's illegal? Anything gonna stick me? Where you coming from today?"

"Get outa my bag," I say. "I didn't give you permission to search it."

"Why not? What are you trying to hide?"

"I know my rights."

"Oh, he knows his rights," says the white cop to the black cop. "A roadside lawyer."

"Where you coming from?" asks the black cop again. He's still holding my bag, still going through it. I don't keep anything illegal in there. I ain't crazy. But he doesn't give a crap about my rights.

"I ain't gotta tell you that."

"Well, looks like you're going to jail then," says the white cop, "since you wanna be combative and not help us out. Gimme that phone." He grabs it out of my hand.

"I wasn't doin' nothin'," I say. "I was just walking."

"Put your hands up against the wall."

"But I was just walking down the street. I didn't break any laws."

Technically speaking, that's not true. I did sort of steal a lady's wallet today. But they don't know that. This is just a straight-up shakedown. Trying to fill their quota.

"You don't wanna work with us, you leave us no choice," says the black cop, and he kicks my feet apart. He's none too gentle about it. He starts patting me down while the white cop gets on his radio.

I know this game. First they hope I'm gonna start crying and cooperate. They must think I'm a kindergartener.

Next, they hope I either run or start fighting. Then they have an excuse to chase me down, beat me up and charge me with a real crime. They get to look like they're doing their job. My brown ass sits in the can until they either decide to charge me or let me go. They don't care. I'm not even a human to them. My freedom, my rights, mean nothing.

They spend a long time going through my stuff. They take the money out of my pocket.

"How'd you earn this money?" asks the white cop. He holds up the twenty bucks I have left after buying breakfast and the phone card.

"I ain't gotta tell you that," I say.

"You get it from selling drugs?"

"No."

"Well, unless you can prove how you got it, I'm gonna seize it as the proceeds of a crime."

"Man…" I'm so angry, my legs are shaking. I'm afraid I'm gonna fall to the ground. But I know if I do that, out come the nightsticks. *Oh, we thought he was trying to crawl away, so we had to use force to subdue him.* "That's my money. You have no right to take it."

"Oh, so you have a job?"

"No, but…"

"Then how did you get it? How'd you get this money?"

I want to pop this cop in the face so bad, I can hardly hold it in. This is what it all comes down to right here. Five hundred years ago they started bringing us over here on ships so they could force us to do their dirty work. Now they got us standing on the corner with our hands on the wall and our legs spread, taking the money out of our pockets.

Meanwhile, people are walking by on the street like the whole thing isn't even happening.

I told you. You haven't seen me before, even though I'm omnipresent. I am every black kid on the street getting his ass beat by the cops, shot down, run to the ground, stomped on, treated like an animal.

And you just keep on walking like it's not even happening.

I'm not the problem here.

You are.

TEN

I'm standing there wondering if I'm gonna spend the rest of the day, or the rest of the week, or maybe the rest of my life, in jail. See, when poor people get arrested and charged, they don't get bailed out. They can't afford it. They stay in jail until the judge decides what to do with them. That can be weeks or months.

And if you get hit with real charges, you don't have a fancy lawyer to get you out of trouble. You get a public defender who has a hundred other people to deal with that day, so he tells you to plea out because the judge is in a hurry. If you waste the judge's time, he's just gonna come down harder on you. Of course you're guilty. If you were innocent, you wouldn't have gotten arrested.

This is how people's lives get turned upside down in an instant, just because they're black and poor. Doesn't matter if you actually did anything. The system needs something to chew on.

Suddenly, I hear another car screech up.

The cops take their hands off me. I don't want to turn around to see who it is. I don't want to risk making any sudden movements. That's a good way to get shot.

There's a lot of yelling going on. There are angry voices. Black voices. "Y'all better" this and "y'all better" that.

The cops start shouting back at whoever is shouting at them. "Do not come any closer! Stay where you are! Keep your hands where I can see them!"

Man, I really, really want to look. Slowly I begin to inch my head around, but I can't see anything.

I feel a hand on my shoulder. Not a cop hand. A friendly hand.

"Yo, Rasheed," someone says.

Finally I feel like I can turn and look.

It's Worm. One of Boss's lieutenants. He's a tall skinny dude with dreads like mine. Looks kinda like Snoop, only not that tall. I saw Snoop from about a quarter-mile away once. Dude is nine feet high. It was like seeing Jesus.

"Sup, Worm," I say.

"Get outa here," Worm says.

"What?"

"You heard me, fool. Bounce. We got this."

I can hardly believe what kind of day this is turning out to be. How is this even possible?

When I turn around, I see how it's possible. I see no less than six Locals standing on the sidewalk and in the street, arms folded, guns in plain view in their waistbands. I have to admit, Locals are a scary sight when they mean business. They all wear sunglasses. They all have big muscles and wear white sleeveless shirts. And they definitely do not care about the law. Around here, they *are* the law.

All these guys showed up for me? I feel like a celebrity.

I grab my bag and take my phone out of the white cop's hand.

"Thanks, pork chop," I say.

You oughta seen the look on his face. He'd like nothing better than to shoot me right then and there. But he is not that crazy, not that stupid.

He knows who really runs this neighborhood. The E Street Locals do, that's who.

"Yo, Rasheed," says Worm. "Boss gonna catch up with you later."

"Word," I say.

I turn and start walking.

After I go about ten yards, I start running. I run like I've never run before. I know those cops might change their mind at any moment.

I run to my hideout behind the Seven. I don't care how bad that dumpster smells. I snuggle up right behind it and pull a cardboard box over myself.

Man, that dumpster stinks. But I've never been so glad to smell garbage in my life.

I pull out my phone. My heart is pounding. I need to relax. I fire up one of my old TV shows. I wish I was in that black-and-white world right now, where nothing bad ever happens and no one ever dies. Everyone is smiling and everything is perfect.

I'm in there for about five minutes. Suddenly the cardboard gets yanked away.

Bright sunlight hits me in the face. I can't see.

A strong hand reaches down and grabs me by the shoulder. It yanks me to my feet. I squint. It's Worm.

"What you doin' back here?" he says. "Man, it stinks."

"Just hidin' from the cops," I say.

"Man, I told you, you ain't gotta worry about them," Worm says. "We run this hood. They know it. Everyone knows it." His eyes narrow. "Everyone except you, seems like."

I shake my head.

"Uh-uh," I say. "I know it."

"You know it. And now you gonna show it. Come on with me, fool. Today is your lucky day."

He grabs me by the arm and pulls me out of the alley. Three more Locals are standing there waiting for us. Behind them is a black Monte Carlo, stereo bumping, doors open. The inside of the car is pitch black. I can't see anything. It's like looking into the gates of hell.

"What do you mean, my lucky day?" I say.

"You gonna get made a Local," says Worm. "Boss says. I dunno why. You ain't done nothin' to deserve it, far as I'm concerned. But Boss speaks."

I think about running again. But that's just crazy. The cops are easy to avoid. The Locals know everything about me. I can never hide from them.

Worm gets into the car on my right. Another Local gets in on my left. The other two get in up front. The car starts moving.

On our way down the street, we pass by my house. I look at it with longing. I never liked that house, but suddenly it's where I want to be. It stands for everything in my life that was ever worth saving.

But the front door is closed, and the screen door has bars on it. So do the windows.

The curtains are drawn tight. Our house is always on lockdown. No one in there can help me. I'm on my own.

Okay. Fine. I can get through this. I can get through anything. I want to start crying, but I know that will just make things worse.

So I grit my teeth and get ready for whatever lies ahead.

ELEVEN

I used to wonder what getting jumped in would be like. I knew it would be bad. One of my main goals in life was to avoid it. But sometimes the things we try the hardest to avoid are the things we sail right into.

We drive down to a house on E Street that I never pass, no matter what. It's the house where the Locals hang out. Just another run-down bungalow with bars on the windows, weeds in the yard, a half-starved pit bull tied up behind a busted fence. There are always people coming and going from that place. I've heard that some of them go in and never come out again.

I would walk ten miles out of my way to avoid this house.

We pull up and get out. I know if I run, I will have to keep running for the rest of my life. And I'm worried about what they'll do to Moms and Daneeka. I'm still so close to home I can see my house from here. They can have them in a minute if they want them.

So I let them take me in.

We go through the house and out the back door to the yard. Four Locals in black do-rags are sitting in lawn chairs. They're playing dominos around a patio table. Boss is one of them. When they see me, they stop playing.

"Sup," he says to me.

I don't say anything. One of the Locals hits me in the back. He doesn't use his hand. It feels like something metal. A gun.

"Boss say sup, you say sup back," says the Local.

"Sup, Boss," I say.

"Five-o was after you," Boss says.

"Yeah, Boss."

"E Street Locals done saved your ass."

I have to admit that's true. No way around it.

"Yeah, Boss."

"Your daddy was a Local. Locals run this hood. Time you face that fact."

"Yeah, Boss."

"You gettin' jumped in, son." He pulls a phone out of his pocket. "Today the first day of the rest of your life." He grins, gold grill shining in the sun.

I don't have a word for the feeling in my stomach right now. I've never felt this way before. All I can think is, I don't want to die.

I stand there for a long time. Boss makes some calls. Locals start showing up at the house. The yard fills with them. Soon there are dozens. They're all standing around looking at me. They all know who I am. I get the feeling more than a few of them know who my daddy was too.

I get pushed into the center of the yard.

There is no speech. No instructions. No whistle blows. They just start.

They come from behind me, from the side, from in front. Their fists fall on me like meteors. I can't do anything against them. I fall to the ground. Then they use their feet.

They just don't stop.

I can feel myself breaking. There is no air down where I am. No sunlight. Nothing but pain. I curl into a ball and wait for it to end.

For the longest time, it doesn't.

Then, suddenly, it does.

The sea of people parts. Sunlight streams in once again. A hand reaches down and pulls me up. I feel as if I've been reborn.

Which, I guess, is the whole point.

Somehow time passes. I don't know how much. A day. Everything hurts, but nothing is actually broken.

I don't get to go home. Someone gives me some food. Barbecued chicken. Someone else gives me a black do-rag and a white muscle shirt. I lie down in a corner of that filthy house and sleep.

Morning comes.

I get taken to the corner on the main drag and dropped off. There is a soldier with me. He sits in an SUV and watches me.

Before I know it, I'm selling crack to crackheads like I've been doing it all my life.

It's simple. They come up to you and tell you how much they want. You look at their missing teeth, their knotted hair, their filthy clothes, and you feel disgust. You don't even want to touch their money. But you do.

You tell a runner what you need. The runner is a little kid. He goes off and comes back with your order. He hands it to you. And you hand it to the crackhead, who was once a human being and is now more like a ghost. These people are the lowest of the low. They are at the worst point in their lives. And the stuff I'm selling is keeping them there.

I hand the money over to the soldier in the suv.

I do this all day. I think about college. I think about Lanaia.

I think about criminal justice.

When I'm out of rock, I get in the suv. We head back to the Locals' house. The lieutenant who was with me hands the money over to Worm. He makes a big show out of counting it. Like I was going to steal from them.

"See you tomorrow," says Worm.

And that's it. I can go home if I want. First day at the office is over.

I walk the fifty yards that separate my old life from my new life. I take the black do-rag off before I go into the house. I have the same conversation again with Daneeka. I make my mom some tea.

I lock myself in my room.

And I take out my phone and dial Officer Friendly.

TWELVE

I told you those Locals are dumb. So dumb they don't even realize that just because I look like a Local doesn't mean I am one. So dumb they don't realize I want nothing more than to hurt them after what they did to my sister.

Maybe you've seen one of those cop shows where they fit a guy up with a wire under his shirt. You don't need those anymore. Not if you have a cell phone. You dial a number, you put the phone back in your pocket, you act like nothing is going on. Whoever is listening can hear everything.

Before I go to the Locals' house the next day, I dial Officer Friendly's number again. I make sure he can hear me talking. I put the phone back in my pocket. I act like nothing is going on.

I told him that if they came to that house, they would find a lot of drugs and a lot of guns. Those are two things the police find very interesting. So this morning a bunch of his cop friends are waiting around the corner. They're going to stage a bust. A bust I helped set up.

Criminal justice.

My code word is *wonderful*. When the cops hear that, they're supposed to come charging in.

I go into the house. I get handed my bag for the day.

"Wonderful," I say.

The lieutenant who hands me the bag is named Dawg. He gives me a funny look. But he doesn't say anything else.

Why haven't they kicked the door in yet?

"Boss wanna see you before you go out," he says.

"Wonderful," I say.

So I get taken once again to the backyard.

No cops yet. Where are they? Is my phone broken? Is the battery dead?

Boss is still sitting in one of those lawn chairs. He looks like he's been awake for three days straight. He's jumpy. His eyes are glazed over. There's a big gun on the table in front of him. A .45-caliber pistol.

"How you like your job?" he says.

"Wonderful," I say.

I can hear engines revving outside. Cars are pulling up outside the house.

"Yeah, well, you gonna have to produce, or else—" He picks up the gun and waves it at me. I think he's going to shoot me right there.

But then there is shouting. I hear a door being knocked in.

And then gunshots.

I don't wait around. The yard is surrounded by a cinder-block wall about six feet high.

"Rasheed!"

I turn. Why? I don't know. I'm not as smart as I think I am, I guess.

Boss is pointing his gun at me.

"You do this?" he asks.

"Hell yes, fool," I say.

"What about your daddy?" he asks.

"What about my sister?" I ask him.

I'm halfway up and over the wall when I hear the shot. Then there are more shots. I feel something hit me.

Then I feel nothing.

For a long time I don't know where I am.

I open my eyes. I can't see anything but light. It's so bright. It should hurt, but it doesn't.

It doesn't hurt because I don't have eyes anymore. I don't have a body. I'm in some weird place. It's not a place on earth. It's a place that doesn't exist.

"Rasheed," says a voice.

It's a voice I haven't heard in a long time.

My pops.

I see his face over me, big and warm. I haven't seen him in a long time, but I would know him anywhere.

He starts talking to me. I can't remember everything he says. I know he says he's sorry. He made some bad choices. Some stupid decisions. But he didn't know what else to do with his life. He did the best he could. He sees now that his best wasn't very good. He wants my forgiveness.

And I give it to him.

He tells me that everything is a choice, even the life you're born into. He chose that life because he had things to learn.

And because he had things to teach. But his life is over now. It's my turn.

That's how I know for sure my daddy is dead. Because I visited him in the afterlife while I was dead myself.

My time is not up yet, he says. I can go back if I want. And I can make my own choices. I don't have to do what other people want for me. What other people have laid out. I can make myself into whatever I want. And he will be watching.

"Do you want to go back?" he asks me.

"Yes," I say.

I can see that I have a lot left to do.

THIRTEEN

If there's one thing I love, it's french fries.

This hospital has great french fries. The rest of their food is terrible. But there's a food court in the lobby, and there's a little place there that sells better food. Real food. Best fries I've had since Officer Friendly took me out to lunch.

That seems like a thousand years ago. Another life. Was it really just a few weeks ago?

When Boss shot me, he almost killed me. That's what he was trying to do.

But it was also the last thing he ever did. Cops came in and took him out right after he pulled the trigger on me. He tried to shoot them too. You can't do that and expect to live very long.

Then they saved my life. They gave me CPR and kept me alive until the ambulance got there.

So I guess the cops are all right after all.

I don't remember any of that. That's when I thought I was in Heaven, talking to my daddy. I still don't know if that was real or a dream. Felt real enough. When I woke up, I felt like he had just been in the room.

The doctors say I am lucky to be alive. The bullet went in through my back and came out through my chest. It took out a lung. They were able to repair that. It missed my spine, which was also pretty lucky. I'm not paralyzed. Not like Neeks. But I came close.

Those Locals were trying to kill all of us, I guess. My whole family.

The cops busted them up pretty good. I guess there was a lot of shooting. Some Locals are dead. Lots more are in jail. It was a bad day for the Locals. A good day for my neighborhood.

And all because of me.

Now I'm sitting here in my wheelchair, with the sun beaming down on me. The doctor said I could go sit outside. I haven't felt fresh air in weeks. I feel like I'm king of the world. I've got a plate full of french fries. And across from me sits Lanaia. What else could I want in life?

"You better eat every one of those fries," she says. "You gotta keep your strength up to get better."

It's the first real food I've eaten since I woke up. I've had two surgeries. Man, it takes a long time to get better when you get shot. It's not like in the movies. You don't just tough it out and keep going. It changes your whole life.

Lanaia and I have been talking. Well, mostly she's been talking. I still don't have a lot of extra energy. But she has plans for me.

I need to get my GED. That's first.

Then I take the SATs and apply to the university. I will have to get money from somewhere, but she says she can help me with that. Turns out there are a lot of ways to find money for school. Scholarships and grants, mostly. I didn't know about any of them. Well, I know now. There are lots of people who will help me if I show them I am willing to try.

Then I start taking classes. Criminal justice. That's what I want to do. I want to help make the world a better place.

The first way I can do that is by changing myself.

The second way is by helping other people.

And the third way is this. If I can't help them, and if they won't change themselves, then they get locked up. Boom. Normal people have a right to a normal life.

There are things about my life that are still not perfect. My mom is still sick. Daneeka will always be paralyzed. I've got a long way to go before I get back on my feet.

But right now I'm alive. I'm sitting in the sunshine, talking to a girl I like and eating french fries. What better way is there to spend an afternoon?

And when it comes down to it, what else do we really have in life except for this moment right now?

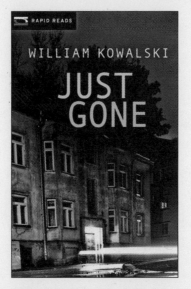

978-1-4598-0327-5 pb, 978-1-4598-0328-2 pdf
978-1-4598-0329-9 epub

Mother Anqelique runs a shelter for homeless mothers and their children in the inner city. When newly orphaned Jamal arrives at the shelter, he tells fantastic stories of a man named Jacky Wacky, who protects the poor children of the city and punishes the adults who harm them. Angelique doesn't believe his stories at first, but strange things begin to happen, and she is forced to admit there are some truths that her faith cannot explain.

"Worthy and positive...and its hopeful message for exploited and abused inner-city youths... Appropriate for adult literacy and ESL programs."
—*Publishers Weekly*

RAPID READS
WWW.RAPID-READS.COM

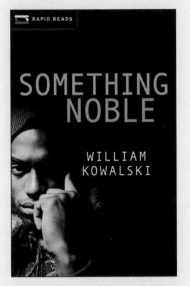

978-1-4598-0013-7 pb, 978-1-4598-0014-4 pdf
978-1-4598-0015-1 epub

Linda is a young, hardworking single mom struggling to get by from paycheck to paycheck. Her son Dre needs a kidney transplant, and the only one who can help Dre is his half-brother LeVon, a drug-dealing gangbanger who thinks only of himself. Somehow Linda must get through to LeVon in order to save her son.

"Linda's voice snags readers' attention with the first sentence…[and] there are several nifty twists…Marked by an authentic plot and realistic characters, this slim volume delivers what it advertises and deserves a bright spotlight."
—*Library Journal*

RAPID READS
WWW.RAPID-READS.COM

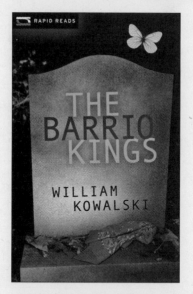

978-1-55469-244-6 pb, 978-1-55469-245-3 pdf
978-1-55469-440-2 epub

2011 Golden Oak Award Nominee
2011 SLJ's Top Book Choices for Youth in Detention List

Rosario Gomez gave up gang life after his brother was killed in a street fight. Now all he wants to do is finish night school and be a good father. But when an old friend shows up to ask him why he left the gang, Rosario realizes he was fooling himself if he thought his violent past would just go away.

"While the story can be seen as a cautionary tale about the dangers of gang life, it's never preachy...Recommended." —*CM Magazine*

RAPID READS
WWW.RAPID-READS.COM